W9-BLL-401

For Teresa, an extraordinary person!

SIMON & SCHUSTER BOOKS FOR YOUNG READERS
An imprint of Simon & Schuster Children's Publishing Division
1230 Avenue of the Americas, New York, New York 10020

Copyright © 2015 by Ben Clanton
All rights reserved, including the right of reproduction in whole or in part in any form.
SIMON & SCHUSTER BOOKS FOR YOUNG READERS is a trademark of Simon & Schuster, Inc.

For information about special discounts for bulk purchases, please contact Simon & Schuster Special Sales at
1-866-506-1949 or business@simonandschuster.com.
The Simon & Schuster Speakers Bureau can bring authors to your live event. For more information or to book an event,
contact the Simon & Schuster Speakers Bureau at 1-866-248-3049 or visit our website at www.simonspeakers.com.
Book design by Lucy Ruth Cummins
The text for this book is set in 2011 Slimtype.
The illustrations for this book are rendered in watercolor and pencil and assembled in Adobe Photoshop.
Manufactured in China
0315 SCP
2 4 6 8 10 9 7 5 3 1
Library of Congress Cataloging-in-Publication Data
Clanton, Ben, 1988- author, illustrator.
Something extraordinary / Ben Clanton.—First edition.
pages cm
Summary: A little boy wants his wishes to come true.
ISBN 978-1-4814-0358-0 (hardcover)
ISBN 978-1-4814-0359-7 (eBook)
[1. Wishes—Fiction. 2. Imagination—Fiction.] I. Title.
PZ7.C52923So 2015
[E]—dc23
2013048732

Something Extraordinary

Ben Clanton

Simon & Schuster Books for Young Readers
New York   London   Toronto   Sydney   New Delhi

I wish I could fly!

And breathe underwater.

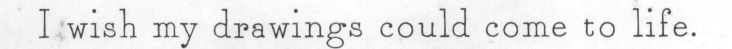

I wish my drawings could come to life.

And that I could move
things with my mind.

I wish the rain came in seven different colors.

And flavors!

I wish that every time I took a
step it would make a funny sound.

oink

toot!

baa

AND I wish I had a BIG bushy tail.

Fangs too!

I really REALLY
wish I could talk
with animals.

And I wish I had an unusual pet.

Or twenty-two!

Or a hundred!

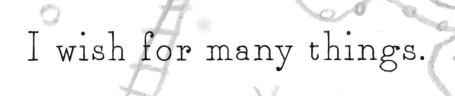

I wish for many things.

But mostly I wish . . .

that *something* would happen.

Something real!

Something . . .

. . . EXTRAORDINARY!